margaret Tempest.

Little Grey Rabbit's Birthday was first published
in Great Britain by William Collins Sons & Co 1944

This edition produced for The Book People Ltd, Hall Wood Avenue,
Haydock, St. Helens, WA11 9UL

Abridged text copyright © The Alison Uttley Literary Property Trust 2000
Illustrations copyright © The Estate of Margaret Tempest 2000
Copyright this arrangement © HarperCollins*Publishers* 2000
Additional illustration by Mark Burgess
Little Grey Rabbit ® and the Little Grey Rabbit logo are
trademarks of HarperCollins*Publishers* Limited

1 3 5 7 9 10 8 6 4 2

ISBN: 0 00 198391 1

The HarperCollins website address is: www.**fire**and**water**.com

Printed and bound in Singapore

LITTLE GREY RABBIT'S BIRTHDAY

ALISON UTTLEY
Pictures by Margaret Tempest

Collins

An Imprint of HarperCollins*Publishers*

SQUIRREL AND HARE were gardening one fine day. "It's little Grey Rabbit's birthday on Midsummer Day," said Squirrel. "We must give her a nice present."

"A very nice present," agreed Hare. "A cake or something. Something we can all share."

"Yes, a birthday cake with candles on it," said Squirrel.

"I don't like the taste of candles," objected Hare.

"They're not to eat!" cried Squirrel. "They are to show how old you are. Three candles if you are three years old."

"And a hundred if you are a hundred years old," said Hare. "Oh, Squirrel, can we make the cake ourselves?"

"I think so," nodded Squirrel. "But it must be a secret."

Just then Grey Rabbit came running out of the house.

"Grey Rabbit," said Hare. "Squirrel and I have been saying that it will be your b-b-"

"Shh! Not a word!" whispered Squirrel.

"No! It's a secret," said Hare hastily.

"A secret from me?" asked Grey Rabbit.

"It's something that mustn't be told," said Hare with importance.

"You are a funny pair," laughed Grey Rabbit. "Will you come for a walk to visit the Speckledy Hen? I want some eggs for tea."

"We'll come, won't we Hare?" said Squirrel, throwing down the rake.

They went through the field where Moldy Warp lived.

"Hello!" he cried when the three friends arrived. "This is a surprise." He hurried to fetch glasses of heather ale and brought them outside.

"I'm going to tell," Hare suddenly exclaimed. "I can't keep the secret in. I shall burst!"

"No! No!" cried Squirrel, shaking his arm.

"Come inside, and whisper it to me and the doorpost," said Mole kindly. Hare followed him into the passage.

"It's Grey Rabbit's birthday on Midsummer Day, and we are going to make a cake," he said breathlessly.

"Ah! That is a good secret!" agreed Mole. "I'll give her a present."

"And come to tea with us," said Hare.

"Thank you, Hare," said Mole.

The three friends said goodbye and Grey Rabbit
led the way through the wood to the great tree
where Owl lived.

Squirrel ran up the tree and called softly through the open window.

"Wise Owl! It's Grey Rabbit's birthday on Midsummer Day."

"Gr-gr-gr," snored Wise Owl, but he heard in his dreams all the same.

They passed into the fields where Hedgehog was coming back from milking.

"Can we have a drink?" asked Squirrel, dancing up to him. "It's thirsty work keeping secrets."

Hare took Old Hedgehog aside and whispered, "It's Grey Rabbit's birthday on Midsummer Day. We are going to make her a cake, and you can come and taste it."

"Ah! Thank ye!" cried Hedgehog.

"Come along, Hare. We shall never get to the Speckledy Hen's house," called Grey Rabbit, "if you spend all the time telling secrets."

When they arrived at the farm, there was the Speckledy Hen walking about.

"We've come for some eggs, Speckledy Hen," said Grey Rabbit.

While the Hen was filling up the basket, Hare whispered in her ear.

"It's Grey Rabbit's birthday on Midsummer Day. We are going to make a cake, and you can come and taste it."

"I'll bring a present for dear Grey Rabbit," whispered Hen.

The next day Squirrel and Hare decided to make the cake.

"We must do it secretly," said Hare. "Won't Grey Rabbit be surprised! She doesn't know we can make cakes."

"We don't know either," muttered Squirrel.

"Grey Rabbit! Go away!" commanded Hare, when little Grey Rabbit came in from the garden.

"Oh Hare! What have I done? What's the matter?" Her ears drooped and a tear came into her eye.

Squirrel stamped her foot. "Hare! How stupid you are!" she exclaimed. She wiped Grey Rabbit's eyes, and said kindly, "Grey Rabbit! Please will you take a bottle of primrose wine to Wise Owl?

He was hooting last night. Moldy Warp would like a visit, and I am sure Fuzzypeg would love to hear a story."

"Then I'll run off at once,"
said Grey Rabbit, smiling
at her two friends.

"Goodbye!" called Squirrel and Hare, and
they waved their paws as Grey Rabbit went
along the lane.

"Quickly! Quickly!"
cried Hare.

Squirrel sniffed at all the jars of spices and herbs on the dresser.

"Here's tansy and woodruff, and preserved violets and bottled cherries," she said.

"Here's poppyseed and acorns and beech nuts," said Hare. "Oh, here's the pepper pot. How much shall I put in?"

"A fistful of everything makes a nice cake," said Squirrel.

So they dipped their paws into every jar, and mixed the seeds and herbs in the yellow bowl.

"Is the oven hot?" said a deep voice. There at the window was Old Hedgehog watching them with twinkling eyes.

"I comed with extra milk for the cake," said he. "You didn't ought to put pepper in it."

Hare blushed and tried to hide the pepper pot.

"Oh Hare! We shall have to begin all over again," said Squirrel.

"I'll come and lend a hand," said Old Hedgehog.

He made up the fire and showed Squirrel how to mix the sugar and butter together and how to sprinkle in the currants and spices.

Hare ran to the garden and brought in rose petals and violets – all the sweet-smelling things he could find to add to the cake. He beat up the eggs till they were a yellow froth, and Hedgehog dropped them into the mixture.

"Now I must be off," said Hedgehog. "Remember not to open the oven door till the good rich smell comes out."

They popped the cake in the hot oven and shut the door.

After a while there came a strong sweet smell.

"The cake!" Hare cried. "It's telling us it's ready to come out."

So Squirrel wrapped a cloth round her paw and lifted out the good-smelling cake, as brown as a berry, all puffed up and crinkly with sugar and spices.

They carried it into the garden and hid it under an empty beehive.

The next day when Grey Rabbit had gone out to gather wool from the hedges, Squirrel ran to the garden for the cake. She iced it and wrote

GREY RABBIT'S BIRTHDAY

on the top in pollen dust.

Hare put lots of candles round the edge – big candles, little candles, red and blue and green ones – and then they danced for joy. "It is fit for a fairy queen," they told each other.

They hid the cake in the beehive again, ready for Midsummer Day.

"I'm going to make a fan for Grey Rabbit," said Squirrel. "I shall ask the green woodpecker and the goldfinch for some feathers."

"And I will make a purse for her," said Hare.

Squirrel begged a few feathers from the birds. She put them together, and there was the prettiest little fan of green and gold.

Hare went to the pasture for a puff-ball. He washed the little bag in the dew, then he tied it with ribbon-grasses.

Darkness came and the three little animals went upstairs to bed.

In the night Grey Rabbit was wakened by a faint noise under her window. She slipped out of bed, and putting her cloak over her nightgown, ran downstairs and into the garden.

There, crouched in a sad, prickly little ball, was Fuzzypeg.

"What's the matter, Fuzzypeg?" whispered Grey Rabbit.

"I comed to say Happy Birthday," said Fuzzypeg. "I got out of the window, and I runned very fast, but I heard Wise Owl hooting, and I got frightened."

"Poor little Fuzzypeg," said Grey Rabbit softly.
"You had better come into my bed."

She took his paw and led him upstairs.

"I knew you'd take care of me, Grey Rabbit. Happy Birthday."

"It isn't my birthday till tomorrow, Fuzzypeg," said Grey Rabbit.

She tucked him up, then she wrapped her cloak round herself and crept under the bed. She couldn't sleep with a bundle of prickles by her side.

The next morning Hare and Squirrel raced downstairs to get the breakfast.

"I'm going to say Happy Birthday to Grey Rabbit," said Hare.

"So am I," said Squirrel.

"I shall say it first because I'm bigger than you," said Hare.

"No, I shall say it first because I'm the little one," said Squirrel.

They stared at each other crossly.

"Let's both say it together," said Squirrel.

So upstairs they bundled, and they flung open the bedroom door.

"Happy Birthday!" came squeaking from the bed, and out of the blankets came Fuzzypeg's dark head.

"I said it first!" said he.

The noise wakened Grey Rabbit, and she crawled out from under the bed.

Hare and Squirrel were so surprised, they never said Happy Birthday at all. They just stared and stared.

"Milk-o!" the call came from the kitchen. "Has anyone seen our Fuzzypeg? He runned away in the night, and it's my belief he came to see Miss Grey Rabbit."

"Here he is, Hedgehog!" they shouted, running downstairs.

"I said it first," boasted Fuzzypeg. "I said Happy Birthday before any of you."

"He said he would be the first and he's done it,'"
said Old Hedgehog proudly.

"Let him stay for breakfast," pleaded Grey
Rabbit, and Hedgehog agreed.

Soon they all sat round the table and ate the
nice food.

"It's your birthday, Grey Rabbit," said Squirrel.
"So you shall have a holiday. We'll wash up the
cups and plates."

"Then I'll go into the garden
with Fuzzypeg and show him
the flowers," said Grey Rabbit.

When they came to the beehive a stream of
honeybees flew out.

"Hare! Squirrel! A swarm of bees is living in
our empty hive," called Grey Rabbit. "Isn't it
exciting? Listen, they are humming something."

This is what they heard:

> "It's Grey Rabbit's Birthday,
> She doesn't want money
> Or fine clothes or riches.
> We'll make her some honey."

Hare and Squirrel looked at one another and
sighed. "Honey out of our cake," they whispered.

At four o'clock Squirrel and Hare sent Grey
Rabbit upstairs, while they got ready the tea.
Then they ran down the garden to the beehive.

They lifted up the straw skep, and there was
the cake, looking nicer than ever. Around it
were little pots of honey, each as big as a thimble.

They carried the treasures indoors and placed
them on the table. Grey Rabbit came running
downstairs.

What a surprise! The table was beautiful with
the birthday cake and all the candles alight upon
it. The tiny pots of honey shone like gold, and
there were dishes of cresses and nuts and cream.

"Oh! Oh!" cried Grey Rabbit. "What's this?"

"It's somebody's birthday cake," said Squirrel.

"It's everybody's cake, and here they come to the feast," said Hare.

Up the path came many little feet. Then there was a rat-tat-tat at the door.

"Come in! Come in!" cried Squirrel.

In trooped Moldy Warp, the Hedgehog family, the Speckledy Hen and a crowd of little animals.

"Many Happy Returns, Grey Rabbit," they cried. They saw the table, the lighted cake and the honey pots.

Then Squirrel gave Grey Rabbit the little fan made of feathers and Hare brought out the purse tied with green ribbon-grass.

Everybody had brought a present, but Moldy Warp's present was the best of all. It was the song of the nightingale in a tiny musical box.

They were all listening to the music, when the door was pushed open and a pair of large blinking eyes appeared.

"I won't come in," hooted Wise Owl, "but I have brought a small token of my regard for Grey Rabbit."

He thrust one claw forward and dropped a book on the table. Then he drifted away as silently as he had come.

"Whew!" exclaimed Moldy Warp. "That was a shock."

"What has he brought?" asked Hare.

"It's called *Wise Owl's Guide to Knowledge*," said Grey Rabbit, holding the tiny green volume.

"Cut the cake, Grey Rabbit!" called Hare. "I'm hungry. Cut the cake!"

So Grey Rabbit cut the beautiful birthday cake
and they all had a piece. It was as nice as it
looked. Really, Hare and Squirrel had made it
very well!

Moldy Warp drank Grey Rabbit's health,
Squirrel recited a little poem, and Hare played a
tune on his flute.

They all laughed and sang and danced till night
came, and then they went home by the light of
the moon.

"What a lovely birthday it has been," said Grey Rabbit. "How kind everybody is to me!"

She looked at all the little treasures the woodland folk had brought.

Then she went upstairs to bed, with the musical box under her arm. She turned the handle and the voice of the nightingale came trilling out. From the woods another nightingale answered.

"A Happy Birthday, Grey Rabbit," it seemed to say. "Thank you for all the fun you give us."